STORIES FROM

JAPAN

Folklore of the World

Each of the Folklore of the World Books contains carefully selected myths and folktales most representative of a single country. These books will help children to understand people in other lands and will help them to develop an appreciation for their customs and culture. Peace for the world can come only through the spreading of this understanding and appreciation.

The Folklore Books are the third step in the Dolch program, *Steps to a Lifetime Reading Habit.* The series on these graded steps, starting with the most elementary, are: the First Reading Books, the Basic Vocabulary Books, the Folklore of the World Books, and the Pleasure Reading Books.

Folklore Books are prepared under the direction of Edward W. Dolch, formerly Professor of Education, University of Illinois. In all the series, emphasis is placed on good storytelling and literary quality, as well as on simplicity of vocabulary.

Books in this series are (to date):

STORIES FROM

Folklore of the World

by EDWARD W. DOLCH
and MARGUERITE P. DOLCH

illustrated by
LUCY and JOHN HAWKINSON

GARRARD PUBLISHING COMPANY
CHAMPAIGN, ILLINOIS

Foreword

The folklore of Japan comes from the olden times when the people of the islands were simple farmers, hunters, and fishermen. These people were ruled over by lords, who had soldiers, some of whom were like the knights of Europe, and were called samurai.

In those days, the people felt that they were surrounded with magic. They felt that there were spirits in the trees, in the animals of the forests, and in the fish of the sea. The people loved stories of magic happenings. At the same time, they told "human stories" of love and work of people. But they had few of the stories of animals acting and talking like human beings that many other countries have. And they had fewer stories of the lives of the gods.

The islands of Japan and the seas about them and the mountains rising above them have always been beautiful, and the Japanese have felt that beauty. Much of this feeling for beauty they have tried to express in their folklore.

If these stories show you the interest of the folklore of Japan, you will want to go to the many books of such stories and enjoy more of them.

E. W. DOLCH

Santa Barbara, California

v

Contents

The Willow Tree

In a village by a river, there grew a very large and beautiful willow tree. All the people of the village loved this willow tree.

The children of the village played in the grass under the willow tree. In the evening, the old men sat under the willow tree and talked of many things.

One day, some men came from the Emperor of Japan.

"The Emperor has sent us to build a bridge across the river," said the men to the people of the village. "We must cut down many trees to build the bridge. We will begin by cutting down the big willow tree that grows by the river."

There was a young farmer who lived in the village. His name was Heitaro. Every morning he walked along the riverbank to his farm. Every evening he walked home and stopped to rest under the willow tree.

Heitaro loved the willow tree very much. His father had stopped to rest under the willow tree on

2

his way home from work. And his grandfather had stopped to rest under the willow tree on his way home from work.

To Heitaro, the willow tree was like one of his family.

When Heitaro heard that the men were going to cut down the willow tree to make the bridge, he went to the men and said,

"I will give you many trees from my farm. But do not cut down the big willow tree that grows by the river."

So the willow tree was not cut down to make the bridge across the river.

One evening, when Heitaro was returning from his work, he stopped by the willow tree. There under the willow tree he saw a beautiful young girl.

Heitaro bowed to the girl, and the girl bowed to him. At first, Heitaro did not know what to say. Then he said,

"The willow tree is very beautiful, is it not?"

"Yes," said the girl. "I am glad that you think that the willow tree is very beautiful."

"The willow tree is very old," said Heitaro.

"But the Spirit of the willow tree will always be young," said the girl.

Then the girl said, "Goodbye," and disappeared. And Heitaro walked home very slowly.

That night Heitaro did not sleep very well. He kept thinking of the beautiful girl under the willow tree. He wanted to see her again and to talk to her. He knew that he was in love with the beautiful girl.

The next morning, Heitaro went to his farm as he did each day. But as he passed the willow tree, he bowed low.

"Willow tree, may I see again here under your branches the beautiful girl that I talked to yesterday?"

In the evening, Heitaro could hardly wait until he came to the willow tree. There was the girl coming toward him with a smile on her face.

"Dear friend," said the girl, "come and sit under the branches of the willow tree and rest."

Heitaro and the beautiful girl sat under the branches of the willow tree many times and talked together.

At last Heitaro told the girl

that he loved her and asked her to be his wife.

"Do you love me so much that you will never ask me about my father and mother?"

"Yes," said Heitaro. "But tell me your name."

"My name is Willow," said the girl.

Heitaro and Willow were married. And in all Japan there was not a happier home.

In a year, Heitaro knew that he was the happiest man in all of Japan. A little son was born. Heitaro and Willow named their little son Higo.

The Temple of
the Goddess of Mercy

Heitaro and Willow were very happy. They were the happiest father and mother in the whole village, for their little son, Higo, was a beautiful child.

When Higo was five years old, the Emperor of Japan sent some men to the village. These men said to the people of the village,

"The Emperor of Japan is going to build a temple in your village. The temple is for the Goddess of

Mercy. It is going to be a very beautiful temple."

The people of the village were very happy. They were glad that the Emperor of Japan was going to build a beautiful temple in the village.

The temple was to be of stone. But many trees were needed to make a wooden roof. The people of the village said to the men who were to build the temple,

"We will give our beautiful willow tree by the river to help make the roof of the temple."

When Heitaro heard that the men were going to cut down the

willow tree, he went to them and said,

"Do not cut down the willow tree. In its place, I will give you many trees from my farm."

So the men did not cut down the willow tree that day.

But the people of the village talked together, and they said,

"We must give the most beautiful thing that we have to the temple of the Goddess of Mercy. And the most beautiful thing that we have in this village is the big willow tree that grows by the river."

Now there was much sadness in the house of Heitaro, for Willow was sick. When she heard that the beautiful willow tree was to be cut down, the tears ran down her face. She could not stop crying.

At last Willow said to Heitaro,

"Six years ago I came to you because you loved the willow tree so much. You did not let the men cut down the beautiful tree to make the bridge over the river. So because of your kindness to the tree, the gods of the sky let me come to earth as a young girl.

"For I am the Spirit of the willow tree. That is why I could not tell you of my father or of my mother.

"My dear husband, take care of our little son, Higo, and tell him that his mother loved him very much."

Heitaro heard Higo crying and went to take him up in his arms. When he looked back, Willow had disappeared.

"Do not cry, little son," he said. "Your mother was the Spirit of the willow tree. When the gods called, she had to go back to the beautiful willow tree that grew by the river."

Then Heitaro and Higo went down to the river. The men had cut down the beautiful willow tree. It lay upon the ground, and the men were cutting off the branches.

But when the men tried to push the great log down to the river so that it would float down to the village, they could not move it.

Then Higo, who was only five years old, put his little hands upon the great log. He patted it and loved it. And when he pushed with his two little hands, the great log, which had been made from the beautiful willow tree, moved slowly down to the river.

Heitaro and Higo stood by the river watching the great log go down to the village.

Heitaro sang a song to Willow to tell her how much he loved her.

Even today, when children are helping with any work, they sometimes sing a song. In the song, they remember how little Higo pushed the great log of the willow tree down to the river.

The Piece of Straw

There was once a young man who had no father and no mother. He had no sister and no brother. He was all alone in the world. And he was very poor.

The poor young man was very unhappy.

One day, he said to himself, "I will go to the temple and pray to the Goddess of Mercy. She will tell me what to do so that I can live a better life."

The young man went to the

temple. He bowed his head to the floor and prayed,

"Dear Goddess of Mercy, help me. Tell me what to do so that I can live a better life. For I have no father or mother to help me."

Three days and three nights the young man prayed. But no message came.

"Goddess of Mercy," prayed the young man, "I will stay on my knees before you until you send me a message."

The priests of the temple said to one another,

"What shall we do? The young

man prays all day. The young man prays all night. If he does not eat, he will die."

So every evening one of the priests brought the young man something to eat. But the young man still prayed day and night to the Goddess of Mercy.

Twenty-one days and twenty-one nights the young man prayed.

At last the young man dreamed that he saw a man with a long white beard.

"I bring you a message from the Goddess of Mercy," said the old man. "Go from the temple and the first thing that you touch will bring good to you."

The young man got to his feet. But he could hardly walk, for he had been on his knees for twenty-one days and twenty-one nights.

As the young man went through the door of the temple, he stumbled and fell. When he picked himself up, he was holding a straw in his hand.

The young man was about to throw the straw away, and then he remembered what the old man with the white beard had said in his dream, "The first thing that you touch will bring good to you."

So the young man held the straw in his hand and went on his way. As he was walking along, a dragonfly came and flew about his head. The dragonfly would not go away, and so the young man caught the dragonfly and tied the straw to his tail.

The young man walked on down the road, holding the straw. The dragonfly flew about at the end of the straw.

Pretty soon, the young man met a woman with a little boy.

"Mother, Mother," cried the little boy. "Please get me the dragonfly tied to the straw."

21

The young man heard the little boy, and he said,

"I will give you the dragonfly." So he gave the little boy the straw with the dragonfly tied to the end.

"Thank you for giving my little boy the dragonfly," said the mother. "May I give you these three oranges in return?"

The young man thanked the woman, took the three oranges, and went on his way.

The young man walked on down the road carrying the three oranges. Soon he met a samurai, or nobleman, who had many servants about him. Some of the servants were carrying a palanquin in which the wife of the samurai was riding. The palanquin was followed by three ladies-in-waiting.

All at once, one of the ladies-in-waiting fainted and fell to the ground.

"Where can we get some water?" cried the samurai. "We must give the lady-in-waiting some water." But no one on the dusty road knew where there was any water.

Then the young man said to the samurai,

"I have these three oranges. Perhaps the juice from these oranges will help the lady."

The lady-in-waiting opened her eyes. She took the juice of the oranges.

"The juice of these oranges has saved my life," said the lady-in-waiting. "I think I would have died if no one had given me a drink."

The samurai was very glad the young man had helped the lady-in-waiting. He had one of his servants give the young man a roll of fine cloth.

The young man thanked the samurai and went on down the road carrying the roll of cloth. He said to himself,

"The Goddess of Mercy has been good to me. The old man with the long beard was right. The straw has brought good to me."

The Beautiful Horse

The young man who had prayed to the Goddess of Mercy was walking down the road. The Goddess of Mercy had given him only a straw. But for the straw he got three oranges. Then for the three oranges he got a roll of fine cloth. The young man carried the roll of fine cloth as he went down the road.

Pretty soon the young man came to some people in the road. Two samurai and their servants were looking down at a beautiful horse that lay in the dust of the road.

One samurai said,

"The horse is dead. Our lord will be very sad, for this was one of his most beautiful horses."

"We must hurry to the castle and tell him that his horse has died," said the other samurai.

The samurai told one of the servants to take the saddle off the beautiful horse. Then they hurried down the road to the castle of their lord.

The young man looked at the horse lying in the dusty road. He thought that it was the most beautiful horse that he had ever seen.

The servant took the saddle off the horse.

"What am I to do with the dead horse?" cried the servant. "I cannot stop to bury it."

The young man looked at the beautiful horse. He wanted to do something for the horse. He did not want the wild animals to eat such a beautiful horse.

"I will give you this roll of fine cloth for the horse," said the young man to the servant.

"Good," said the servant, and

he took the roll of cloth and went on down the road.

The young man sat down in the dusty road by the horse. He put his hand on the horse's soft nose.

"Poor thing," he said, "I think you must have been the most beautiful horse in the whole world."

The horse slowly moved his head.

The young man was surprised and jumped to his feet.

The horse opened its big eyes and looked at the young man.

"You are not dead," cried the young man, and he ran off to find some water for the horse. He found a well in a field with a bucket near it. He brought the bucket full of water and got the horse to drink.

When the horse had had a good drink of water and had rested, it got to its feet. Then the young man went on down the road. The beautiful horse followed him.

It was getting dark. The young man came to a house. He could hear a woman crying.

"My brother is sick, and he is going to die," cried the woman.

Then a man's voice said,

"We cannot go to him, for it is a long way to your brother's house."

"Oh, if only we had a horse," cried the woman, "we could get to his house before he dies."

The young man was very sorry for the woman. He went up to the door of the house. He called out in a loud voice,

"Here is a horse."

A man came out of the house. He looked at the beautiful horse.

"Will you let us have this horse?" he asked.

"Yes," said the young man. "Then your wife can see her brother before he dies."

"We will go right away," said the man. "Will you take care of and use this house and land until I bring your beautiful horse back?"

The young man said he would be glad to take care of the house and the land. The man and his wife both got on the horse and rode off into the night.

The man and his wife never came back.

The young man married a beautiful girl. He and his wife lived in the house by the road and were very happy.

The Girl
with the Wooden Bowl

The old people tell the story of the Girl with the Wooden Bowl.

A long, long time ago, there lived a poor widow with one daughter. This daughter was very beautiful.

One day the widow became sick. She knew that she was going to die. She called her daughter to her and said,

"My dear child, I am going to go to meet your father. You will be alone, and I want no harm to come to you. Put this wooden bowl upon your head. Keep it there. When the right time comes, you can take it off. Then you will be happy all the rest of your life."

The girl put the big wooden bowl upon her head. The bowl covered all of her beautiful hair. It covered most of her beautiful face. No one could see how beautiful she was.

The mother seemed happy. She closed her eyes and went to sleep. In the morning, she did not wake up. The girl knew that her mother had died.

At first the people in the village were good to the girl, who was all alone in the world. They gave her work. And they tried to take the big wooden bowl off her head.

"No," said the girl. "You must not take the bowl off my head. Before my mother died, she told me that I must wear this big wooden bowl on my head."

The boys and girls of the village began to laugh at the girl with the bowl on her head. So the girl went out to the country-side to work in the rice fields. The other workers laughed at her. Some of them tried to take the bowl off her head. But she was a good worker, and pretty soon a rich farmer asked her to work in his rice fields.

The girl was kind and gentle to everyone. The farmer's wife became sick. The farmer asked the girl with the bowl on her head to come to his house and look after his wife.

The girl with the bowl on her head looked after the farmer's wife as if she were her own mother.

Now it so happened that the farmer and his wife had a fine son. The son had gone to the city. But one day the son came home to the farm.

The son asked his mother about her servant. The mother could tell him nothing but that the girl was kind and gentle. And she always wore the wooden bowl on her head.

The more the son saw of the girl with the bowl on her head, the more he liked her. She was always kind and gentle.

The son did not go back to the city. He stayed on the farm and helped his father with the rice fields. One day he said to his father,

"I am in love with the girl with the bowl on her head. I wish to make her my wife."

The father was pleased, for he knew that the girl was kind and gentle. She would make a good wife for his son.

At last the mother saw that the son was really in love with the girl with the bowl on her head. So the father and the mother told their son that he could ask the girl to marry him.

But when the son asked the girl to marry him, the girl with the bowl on her head said, "No." She did not think that the boy's mother would be happy if he married a servant.

Then one night the girl's mother came to her in a dream. She smiled at her daughter and said,

"Marry the farmer's son and all will be well."

So when the farmer's son told her again how much he loved her, the girl said, "Yes," she would marry him.

Now the girl tried to take the big wooden bowl off her head. But she could not get it off. No one could get the bowl off the girl's head.

The girl with the big bowl on her head began to cry.

"Do not cry," said the farmer's son. "I love you with the bowl on your head. And I want you to be my wife."

The people from all over the country-side came to the wedding. The bride's dress was beautiful. But she looked very funny with the big wooden bowl on her head.

In a Japanese wedding, there were three glasses of wine, one little glass, one middle-sized glass, and one large glass. The bride is to take three little drinks of wine from each glass.

As the girl with the bowl on her head took a little drink of wine from the smallest glass, there was a great noise. The bowl on her head broke into two pieces and fell to the floor.

The two pieces of the bowl lay upon the floor, and each piece was filled with gold.

Everyone at the wedding looked down at the gold on the floor. But the farmer's son looked at the face of his bride for the first time. She was the most beautiful girl in all of Japan.

The Two Brothers

Once upon a time there were two brothers. One brother liked to fish, and he was called the Good Fisherman. One brother liked to hunt, and he was called Happy Hunter of the Mountains.

One day Happy Hunter said to his brother,

"Give me your fishhook and let me go fishing."

Now the Good Fisherman had a magic fishhook. And he did not want to give the magic fishhook to his brother.

Happy Hunter said,

"Here is my bow and arrow. Take them and you will enjoy hunting in the mountains."

At last the Good Fisherman gave his magic fishhook to his brother. He took the bow and arrows and went off to the mountains. He hunted all day long. He did not get a thing. And when he came home in the evening, he had nothing to cook for his supper.

Happy Hunter got into a boat and went out to the sea to fish. All day long he fished and he caught nothing. He even lost the

magic fishhook. He did not know
what to do.

At last, when it was dark,
Happy Hunter went home. He said
to his brother,

"I caught no fish. I even lost
your fishhook in the sea."

The Good Fisherman was very
angry.

"It was foolish of you to try to
do something that you did not
know how to do. I shall never
forgive you until you bring my
fishhook back to me."

Happy Hunter was very sad.
He took his sword and broke it
into pieces. Each piece of his

sword he made into a fishhook. He took all the fishhooks to his brother. But the Good Fisherman would not take them.

"I will not forgive you," said the Good Fisherman, "until you bring back to me my magic fishhook that you lost in the sea."

Happy Hunter was very sad. He went down to the sea. The waves of the sea rolled up on the sand, and he knew that he could never find a fishhook in that great sea.

As Happy Hunter sat on the sand an old, old man came up out of the sea.

"I am the Old Man of the Sea," said the man from the water. "Why are you so sad, my boy?"

"My brother will never forgive me," said Happy Hunter. "For I shall never be able to find his magic fishhook that I lost in the sea."

"The King of the Sea is the only one who can help you," said the Old Man of the Sea.

"When I was a child, my grandmother told me about the King of the Sea," said the Happy Hunter. "But no man knows how to get to his palace."

"I will make a magic basket for you," said the Old Man of the Sea. "The magic basket will take you to the palace of the Sea King."

Happy Hunter and the Old Man of the Sea cut many pieces of bamboo.

The Old Man of the Sea made a big basket out of the bamboo. When the basket was finished, he put it into the sea. Then the Happy Hunter got into the basket.

"Goodbye, my friend," said the Old Man of the Sea. "And may you have a safe journey to the palace of the King of the Sea."

The magic basket went over the sea. Pretty soon the magic basket went down under the sea. But the Happy Hunter did not get wet at all. The basket carried the Happy Hunter down to the bottom of the sea.

The Happy Hunter was much surprised to find a beautiful world under the sea. He saw many colored fish swimming among the trees. He saw a road leading to a beautiful palace. He knew that this beautiful palace must be the palace of the King of the Sea.

The King of the Sea

The Happy Hunter walked up the road to the gate of the palace of the King of the Sea. But the gate to the palace was closed.

Beside the gate there was a well. And beside the well grew a beautiful tree. The Happy Hunter knew that before long someone would come to the well to get some water. So the Happy Hunter climbed up into the tree. He could look right down into the well.

Pretty soon the gates of the palace opened. A beautiful girl carrying a golden bucket came to the well. As she was about to put her bucket into the well, she looked down and saw the face of a young man in the water.

With a cry, the young girl dropped her bucket. She looked up into the tree and right into the face of the Happy Hunter.

The beautiful girl ran back to the palace. She ran to the room where the King of the Sea sat on his great chair made of shells.

"Father! Father!" cried the girl, "there is a handsome young man in the tree beside the well."

"We must go and welcome the man to our palace," said the King of the Sea. "For a hundred years or more no man from the Kingdom of Japan has come to visit us."

The King of the Sea and his daughter found the Happy Hunter standing by the well.

"Welcome to our land under the sea," said the King.

The Happy Hunter bowed low. "The Old Man of the Sea told me that only the King of the Sea could help me," he said.

"I will do anything that I can for you," said the King of the Sea.

Then the Happy Hunter told him how he had lost his brother's magic fishhook.

"Father," cried the young princess. "The fishes of the sea can find the magic fishhook."

"Yes," said the King. "I will call all the fishes of the sea. And they will find the magic fishhook."

All the fishes of the sea came to the palace of the King of the Sea. There were big fish and little fish. There were blue fish and yellow fish and red fish. There were fish of all colors.

The King of the Sea asked them all if anyone had seen the magic fishhook. But no fish had seen the magic fishhook.

The big gray fish spoke.

"The Red Lady is not here," he said. "She is sick with a sore throat."

"Go and bring the Red Lady to me," said the King of the Sea.

When the fish who was called the Red Lady came before the King of the Sea, she looked very sick. And when the King of the Sea looked into her throat, he found the magic fishhook.

Very carefully, the King took the fishhook out of the throat of the Red Lady. He gave it to the Happy Hunter.

"Here is your magic fishhook," said the King. "But will you not stay with us for a while?"

So the Happy Hunter did not go back to his country right away. He fell in love with the Princess and they were married.

But after three years had gone by, the Happy Hunter wanted to see his brother again. When he told the King of the Sea that he wanted to take the magic fishhook back to the Good Fisherman, the King of the Sea said,

"It is true that a man always wants to go back to his country. We know that he will not want to live always under the sea."

So Happy Hunter went back to his own village. He gave his brother back the magic fishhook. The Good Fisherman was willing to forgive his brother, and they were happy together again.

But every night the Happy Hunter would go down to the sea. Then the daughter of the King of the Sea would come and sit beside him and talk with him.

Momotaro,
the Peach Boy

One day, an old woman was washing clothes by the river. She beat her clothes on a flat stone, and then let the water run through them.

The old woman and her husband were very poor. Every day the old man went to the forest. All day long he cut wood. At night when he came back to the hut, he was very tired.

The old woman was thinking of her husband as she washed the clothes in the river. He was getting very old. Pretty soon, he would be too old to go to the forest and cut wood.

"If only the gods had given us a little son," said the old woman to herself. "A son would have looked after us when we're old."

There were tears in the old woman's eyes as she washed her clothes in the river.

The old woman looked up the river and she thought she saw a big, big peach floating on the water. The old woman looked again.

There was a big, big, big peach floating on the water. It was the biggest peach that the woman had ever seen. And it was coming toward her.

"Oh! Oh! Oh!" cried the old woman, "I must get that big peach for my husband."

The old woman was afraid that the peach would float by her and go down the river. She sang a little song to the peach,

"The waters far away are salty.
The waters near to me are sweet.
Stay away from the salty water.
Come where the water is sweet."

The old woman sang the song again and again.

The big, big, big peach came nearer and nearer. It stopped at the old woman's feet.

The old woman picked up the peach. She carried it home. And when her husband came home in the evening, she said,

"My dear husband, I have a big surprise for your supper." And she showed him the peach.

The old man looked at the peach and said,

"I never saw such a big peach before. Where did you get it?"

"I saw the big peach floating on the river. I sang a song to the peach and it came right to my feet," said the old woman.

"Well! Well! Well!" said the old man. "I will get a knife and cut the peach so that we can eat it."

But when the old man started to cut the peach, he heard a cry, "Do not hurt me. Do not hurt me."

The big, big, big peach opened. A little boy rolled out on the floor.

"The gods sent me to you because you wanted a son," said the little peach boy.

"Yes! Yes!" cried the old woman.

"We will call you Momotaro, the son of a peach," said the old man.

The Northeastern Sea

Momotaro, the Peach Boy, grew up to be a fine boy. When he was fifteen years old, he came to the old woodcutter and said,

"You have been a good father to me. But now I must go away. I must go to the Northeastern Sea where a wicked Ogre lives upon an island. This wicked Ogre keeps many people in his prison. And this Ogre has a castle filled with treasure. I am going to kill the wicked Ogre and set the people free. I will bring back the treasure to you."

The old woodcutter knew that Momotaro was not like other boys, and so he said,

"My blessing goes with you, my son. Kill the Ogre and set the people free. But. be sure that no harm comes to you."

The old woman made Momotaro some rice cakes to take with him. And the Peach Boy started upon his journey.

All day long, Momotaro walked over the mountains. He got very tired and at last he sat down under a pine tree. He ate one of his rice cakes. A big Dog came out of the forest.

"Give me a rice cake or I will eat you up," said the Dog.

"Ho! Ho!" laughed Momotaro. "I am the Peach Boy. I am on my way to kill a wicked Ogre. And I give a rice cake only to a friend."

When the big Dog heard that he was speaking to the Peach Boy, he bowed his head to the ground.

"I want to be your friend and go with you," he said.

So Momotaro gave the Dog a rice cake.

Momotaro, with the Dog at his side, started on his journey again. Now he walked over the hills and he walked through the fields.

In the morning, Momotaro, with the Dog at his side, met a Monkey.

"Blessings to you, Momotaro," cried the Monkey. "I have heard that you were on your way to kill the wicked Ogre who lives on the island in the Northeastern Sea. I wish to go with you."

"I am going to help the Peach Boy," said the Dog. "We do not need a Monkey to help us."

The Dog was going to fight with the Monkey. But the Monkey

jumped on the Dog's back and hurt him.

"Do not fight," said Momotaro. "You can both be my friends and help me." And he gave the Monkey a rice cake.

The Peach Boy and the Dog and the Monkey went on together.

As they were crossing a field, a beautiful Pheasant walked out in front of them.

At once the Dog wanted to catch the Pheasant. But the Pheasant did not run away. It turned on the Dog.

"Such a brave bird can help us fight the Ogre," said Momotaro.

And he gave the Pheasant a rice cake.

The Pheasant was very happy to go along with Momotaro. The Dog and the Monkey and the Pheasant became good friends.

At last they all came to the Northeastern Sea. Momotaro found a ship to take them to the island where the Ogre lived.

At first, the Dog and the Monkey and the Pheasant were afraid to get on the ship. But Momotaro said,

"You are not afraid of the wicked Ogre. Why be afraid to go on a ship on the sea?"

So they all got on the ship.
Momotaro put up the sail. Away
they went over the ocean. In two
days, the Peach Boy and his
friends came near the island where
the Ogre lived.

Momotaro and the Ogre

When Momotaro saw the island where the Ogre lived, he said to the Pheasant,

"Fly to the castle of the Ogre. Tell him to set free his prisoners or we will come and take his castle."

The Pheasant flew to the island and then to the castle. He sat on the gate of the castle. He called in a loud voice,

"Set free the prisoners. Set free the prisoners."

The Ogre heard the noise. But when he saw that it was only a

75

bird that was making all the noise, he laughed and laughed.

"We will kill you and take your castle. We will kill you and take your castle," cried the Pheasant.

But the Ogre only laughed. He told his servants to kill the bird that was making so much noise. The servants got stones and threw them at the bird. But the Pheasant flew around and around over their heads and no one could hit him.

The ship, with Momotaro and the Dog and the Monkey, got to the island. They could see the castle. There was a high wall

around it. It would be very hard
to get into the castle.

Momotaro and the Dog and the
Monkey walked toward the castle.
They came to a little river. Two
beautiful girls were washing clothes
beside the river. They were crying.

"Why do you cry?" asked
Momotaro.

"We are servants of the Ogre.
The Ogre carried us away from
our father's palace. And one day
he will kill us." And the girls
began to cry again.

"Do not cry," said Momotaro.
"My friends and I will help you.

Show us how to get into the castle of the Ogre."

The girls took Momotaro and the Dog and the Monkey to the back of the castle. There was a little door in the wall. But Momotaro was now such a big man that he had a very hard time to get through the little door.

Momotaro and his two friends ran through the castle. They found the Pheasant fighting the servants of the Ogre. Momotaro and his friends fought the servants too. They fought so hard that they threw all the servants of the Ogre over the castle wall.

Now the Ogre was very much afraid. He knew that Momotaro was too strong for him. He went down on his knees and bowed his head.

"Please, please do not kill me," cried the Ogre, putting his face to the ground.

Momotaro laughed at the Ogre. The Ogre thought Momotaro was going to kill him.

"Let me go, and I will give you all the treasure that is in the castle," cried the Ogre.

Momotaro told the Monkey to tie up the Ogre. Momotaro was going to take the Ogre back to

Japan where he could be put in a strong prison so he could not hurt anyone any more.

Then Momotaro and the Dog and the Pheasant went through the castle. They set free all the prisoners. These people carried the Ogre's treasure down to the ship. Then the people got on the ship too. Momotaro put the Ogre, who was all tied up, in the bottom of the ship.

When all was ready, Momotaro put up the sail and off they all went to Japan. It was a happy homecoming. The father of the two beautiful girls who had helped

Momotaro, put the Ogre in his prison. He never harmed anyone again.

There was a great parade. Momotaro and the Dog and the Monkey and the Pheasant marched at the head of the parade.

The old woodcutter and his wife were very proud of their Peach Boy. Momotaro gave them so much of the Ogre's treasure that they had everything that they wanted for the rest of their lives.

My Lord Bag of Rice

Once upon a time, there was a brave samurai in Japan who was always called "My Lord Bag of Rice." This is the story of why he was called by that name.

The people of the village have forgotten what this samurai's real name was. They would say, "My Lord Bag of Rice is a brave man," or "My Lord Bag of Rice is a kind man." Everyone thought well of My Lord Bag of Rice.

Now it so happened that when this brave man was young, he

went on a journey. He came to a
bridge over a river, which ran on
into a lake nearby. Right in the
middle of the bridge lay a dragon.

The dragon seemed to be
sleeping, and the young man
wanted to go on with his journey.
So the young man stepped right
over the dragon.

Just as he stepped over the
dragon, the young man heard
someone say,

"My brave young man, will you
help me?"

The young man looked up and
saw a dwarf standing on the bridge
before him. On his head was a

crown that looked like the head
of a dragon. And the dragon who
had been lying on the bridge was
gone.

The young man was surprised,
but he asked,

"Did you call to me?"

"Yes," said the dwarf. "For
many days I have been lying on
the bridge in the shape of a
dragon, but no one has been brave
enough to step over me. Just now
you did. And I need a very brave
man to help me."

"I will help you if I can," said
the young man. "Who are you and
what do you want with me?"

"I am the Dragon King, and my palace is under this bridge. I have an enemy who comes down from the mountains and catches my children. That enemy is a giant centipede. Only a man who is not afraid can kill the giant centipede."

"I will help you," said the young man. "Tell me where I may find the giant centipede. I shall shoot the giant centipede with my bow and arrow."

"It is best that you wait until the evening," said the Dragon King. "The giant centipede comes to my palace every evening and takes one of my children back to the mountains."

The Dragon King took the young man to his palace under the bridge. The young man had never seen anything so beautiful. A feast was put before him.

All at once, there was a great noise as if many men were marching.

"The centipede is coming," cried the Dragon King.

"Bring me my bow and arrows," said the young man, "I will kill him." But as he took his bow and arrows, he saw that he had only three arrows left.

The Dragon King and the young man went back and stood on the bridge. They looked toward the mountains. The giant centipede was coming down the mountain.

The young man shot an arrow that hit the centipede in the head. But the arrow did not even hurt the centipede. The centipede kept coming down the mountain.

The young man shot another arrow at the giant centipede and hit him in the head. But the arrow did not even hurt the centipede. It kept coming on toward the bridge.

"You are a brave young man," cried the Dragon King. "But you cannot kill the centipede."

Then the young man remembered a magic that he had known as a child. When you want to be sure to hit something, wet the point of the arrow with your mouth. So the young man put the point of the last arrow into his mouth.

The giant centipede was almost to the bridge.

Then the young man took his last arrow, the point of which he had put into his mouth. He drew his bow back and shot the arrow.

The arrow hit the centipede in the eye and killed it.

There was a great noise. There was a sudden darkness over the lake. When the darkness passed, there was the body of the giant centipede in the waters of the lake.

The Dragon King and all his family came and looked at the dead centipede. Then they all bowed down before the young man.

"You are the bravest man in all Japan," cried the Dragon King.

The Dragon King wanted the young man to stay with him. But the young man said that he must be going home.

A large fish came out of the lake. The Dragon King turned the fish into a man, for it was his servant.

The servant carried a bag of rice. No matter how much rice was taken out of the bag, the bag was always full.

The servant carried the magic bag of rice to the young man's house, and then disappeared.

From that day on, no one in the young man's village was ever hungry, for the young man shared his rice with everyone.

Little One-Inch

Once upon a time, a Mother had a baby boy no bigger than her little finger. She called her baby, Little One-Inch.

Little One-Inch never grew any bigger than a chopstick with which a little boy eats his rice. Little One-Inch ate his rice from doll dishes. His Mother made him clothes which were no bigger than doll clothes.

All the boys in the village made fun of Little One-Inch. They called him Little Finger, and tried to get him to fight. But Little One-Inch only laughed at them.

One day, Little One-Inch said to his Mother,

"It is time I left this village. I want to go to the big city."

"I am afraid you will be hurt if you go to the big city," said his Mother, for she thought that one so small could not take care of himself.

"I can take care of myself," said Little One-Inch. "Please give me a sharp needle, a small wooden soup bowl, and a chopstick."

Little One-Inch put the sharp needle in his belt like a sword.

He said goodbye to his Mother. He carried the small wooden soup bowl down to the river.

There he put the wooden soup bowl into the water. He got into the soup bowl, and he used the chopstick to push the boat from the shore. Away he went down the river.

Sometimes the sun shone. Sometimes the rain came down. But Little One-Inch floated down the river, pushing with the chopstick to keep his bowl away from other things floating in the water.

Pretty soon, Little One-Inch, in his soup bowl, came to the city of

Kyoto, where a great Prince lived. The soup bowl came to the shore, and Little One-Inch got out. He started to walk down a street. But there were so many people that he thought they might step on him. So he hid behind a stone and watched the people go by.

Little One-Inch was getting very hungry. He said to himself,

"I must find some good man who will let me work for him."

So Little One-Inch began to walk along, close to the stone wall. If he stayed very close to the wall, no one would step on him. At last he came to a gate. He went through the gate and found himself in a beautiful garden. He walked up to a big house and stood before the door.

"Here I am," Little One-Inch called out, "I want to see the lord of the house."

A servant opened the door. But he could see no one at the door.

"Here I am," called out Little One-Inch.

The servant looked down on the ground. He saw the clogs that his lord put on his feet when he went out. Beside the clogs, and no higher than they were, he saw a boy.

The servant was frightened. He shut the door and went to call the Prince.

The Prince came to the door. When he saw Little One-Inch beside his clogs, he said,

"Who are you? And what do you want?"

"I am Little One-Inch. And I want to work for you and be your servant."

The Prince was very much pleased to have so small a servant. The Prince gave Little One-Inch to his daughter, the Princess. The Princess thought that Little

One-Inch was the best doll she had ever had.

The Princess and Little One-Inch played many games together. And Little One-Inch loved the Princess very much.

The Princess grew up to be a beautiful lady. Little One-Inch grew too, but not very much. He was a very handsome young man, but he was no taller than your hand.

The Princess and the Ogre

One day the Princess and Little One-Inch went to a temple. When they were coming out of the temple, the Princess saw an Ogre hiding behind a tree.

The Ogre was an ugly-looking giant. He was almost as green as the tree. And he carried a magic hammer. He stepped out from behind the tree, and the Princess was so frightened that she fainted.

Little One-Inch was not afraid.

He stepped in front of the Princess and faced the Ogre.

"Do not hurt the Princess," he cried, as he took out his needle and held it in front of him like a sword.

When the Ogre saw the little man at his feet he laughed and laughed.

"I will eat you with one bite," cried the Ogre. And the Ogre picked up Little One-Inch and swallowed him whole.

Little One-Inch found himself in the Ogre's stomach. It was very dark. Little One-Inch went to work with his needle. He stuck his needle into the Ogre's stomach. He stuck his needle in again and again.

"Ouch! Ouch! Ouch!" cried the Ogre. "My stomach. My stomach. It hurts, it hurts."

The Ogre gave a great cough. He coughed Little One-Inch right up into his mouth. Little One-Inch climbed up into the inside of the Ogre's nose. He stuck the Ogre's nose with his needle, again and again.

"Ouch! Ouch! Ouch!" cried the Ogre. He hit his nose with his big hand, and Little One-Inch fell out of his nose and down to the ground. He fell on some grass and so he did not hurt himself.

The Ogre ran away as fast as he could.

The Princess, who had fainted, now opened her eyes and looked around.

"What has happened?" said the Princess. "I thought I saw a dreadful Ogre behind the trees."

Little One-Inch ran to the Princess.

"Everything is all right now," he said. "The Ogre is gone."

"Little One-Inch, you are very brave," said the Princess. "There really was an Ogre behind the trees, and you must have made him go away."

The Princess looked around and she saw the magic hammer on the ground.

"Look! Look!" cried the Princess. "The Ogre dropped his magic hammer."

The Princess picked up the magic hammer.

"Little One-Inch, what do you wish for most in all the world? For when I hit the magic hammer on the ground, your wish will come true."

"I wish to be as big as other men," said Little One-Inch.

The Princess hit the ground with the magic hammer. There stood beside her a handsome young man, taller than she was.

"Thank you, my Princess," cried the young man. "I will never be Little One-Inch again. For now I am taller than you are."

The Prince was very happy that Little One-Inch had been so brave and had saved his daughter from the Ogre. The Prince was happy, too, that Little One-Inch had become such a handsome young man.

The Princess told her father that she loved the young man. So the two were married and lived happily every after.

The Soldier's Sweetheart

Once upon a time, there was a castle by a river. There were many soldiers to guard the castle. And among the soldiers was a fine-looking young man whose name was Chugoro.

Every evening, Chugoro liked to walk down by the river. The water of the river was very deep where it ran under a bridge. As the young man looked into the deep water, he thought he saw the face of a beautiful girl.

One evening, as Chugoro stood on the bridge, looking into the water, he heard a sound beside him. Looking around, a saw a beautiful girl, dressed in rich silks.

"Will you take a walk with me?" said the girl. "I have something to tell you."

So Chugoro and the girl walked along the bank of the river.

"I have watched you, Chugoro, for a long time," said the girl. "And I wish to have you for my husband."

The girl was very beautiful and Chugoro said that he would marry her.

"You must come with me," said the girl. "And you must not be afraid."

The girl took Chugoro by the hand and walked into the deep water of the river. Chugoro did not know where he was going, but he was not afraid. He closed his eyes, and when he opened them, he was in a beautiful palace.

Every evening, Chugoro met his wife on the bridge over the river. And every evening, the beautiful wife took him to her palace under the river.

"Promise me, my dear husband," she said, "that you will never tell anyone where you go each evening. For if you tell anyone of our marriage, a great unhappiness will come to us."

For a year and a day, Chugoro went every evening to meet his wife. But every evening, he walked more slowly to the bridge over the river.

Chugoro was sick, and he did not know what was the matter with him. His face was white, and he could hardly walk.

Among the soldiers at the castle, there was an old soldier who was a good friend to Chugoro. He had known Chugoro when he was a boy.

This old soldier was very much worried over the way Chugoro looked. He knew that the young soldier was sick. He also knew that Chugoro went away from the castle every evening and did not come back until the sun was beginning to come up.

So one evening, when Chugoro started to leave the castle, the old soldier followed him and spoke to him.

"Chugoro, my boy, I have watched you go away from the castle each evening. And you do not come back until the sun is coming up. You are not getting sleep, and you are making yourself sick."

"Come with me, my friend," said Chugoro, "and I will tell you a strange story. But you must never tell anyone what I am going to tell you."

Then Chugoro told his old friend the story of his wife and how much he loved her. He told his old friend about her palace under the river where he went each night.

The old soldier was very much worried. He knew that Chugoro had married a spirit. And he did not think that it was a good spirit, for she had made Chugoro very sick.

The old soldier said, "I shall never tell anyone what you have told me as long as you are alive. Go to your wife. But be careful, for I am afraid that she is not a good spirit."

Chugoro went to the bridge over the river. But his wife did not come to him.

Chugoro was so sick that he could hardly get back to the castle. He went to his old friend and said,

"I broke my promise when I told

you about my wife. She will never come to me again."

Chugoro lay down on his bed. In the morning he could not get up. A doctor was called. But the doctor could do nothing for him. Chugoro died.

Then the old soldier told the doctor the story that Chugoro had told to him.

"It is not the first young man that she has killed," said the doctor. "For hundreds of years a bad spirit has lived under the bridge. She falls in love with a young man, and then she kills him."

"Chugoro said that she was a very beautiful girl and that she lived in a beautiful palace under the water," said the old soldier.

"This bad spirit may be very beautiful at night," said the doctor. "But in the daytime she sits under the bridge. She looks like a great big frog."

Urashima

Urashima was a young man who
went fishing every day. When he
came home at night, he always
brought a fine fish to his mother
and father. He brought them
money too. For Urashima always
had fish to sell in the village.

One day, Urashima went fishing.
He rowed his boat over the waves,
and then he put down his lines.
But Urashima did not catch any
fish.

At last Urashima felt something

pull on one of his lines. He quickly pulled in his line. He had caught a big turtle.

Now some turtles are a hundred years old. They are said to be servants of the King of the Sea. Urashima had no fish to take home, but he felt it was wrong to kill the turtle. So he let the turtle go back into the sea.

The sun was hot and Urashima was tired. He almost went to sleep. Then he heard someone calling, "Urashima, Urashima."

Urashima saw the turtle that he had put back into the sea. It was swimming around his boat and calling to him.

Urashima spoke to the turtle.

"Do you want to get caught in my fishlines again?" he asked.

"No," said the turtle. "I have come back to thank you for being kind to me. You did not hurt me when I got caught in your fish lines."

"Am I dreaming, or can a turtle really talk?" asked Urashima.

"I can talk," said the turtle. "And I can take you to the palace of the Sea King if you want to go there."

Urashima looked at the turtle and laughed.

"You are just a little turtle," he said, "and I am a big man. How could you take me to the palace of the Sea King?"

"Watch me," said the turtle.

Then right before Urashima's eyes, the turtle grew and grew. Soon it was as big as Urashima's boat.

"Get on my back," said the turtle, "and I will take you to the palace of the Sea King."

Urashima got on the back of

the turtle. The turtle went over the sea as fast as the wind. Then all at once, it went down under the sea.

Urashima saw the fishes swimming around him. Some were big. And some were little. The fish were all the colors of the rainbow. Urashima saw that they bowed before the turtle.

But most surprising of all was that Urashima did not get wet. He was living under the sea just as he used to live in his own village.

At last the turtle came to a beautiful gate. The keeper of the gate was a large, gold-colored fish.

"Welcome home," said the keeper of the gate to the turtle.

"Take this man to the King of the Sea," said the turtle.

When Urashima looked around, the turtle had disappeared. Urashima went into the gate of the palace. He found himself walking down a long hall, and the golden fish was going along beside him.

Soon they came to the throne room of the palace. The King of the Sea was seated on a high throne made of the most beautiful shells. Beside him sat the most beautiful girl that Urashima had ever seen. She was the Princess of the Sea.

The Princess of the Sea

The King of the Sea sat upon his beautiful throne of shells. The Princess of the Sea sat beside him.

"Father," said the Princess, "this is the man who did not hurt the turtle."

Urashima bowed low before the King of the Sea.

"Welcome to the palace of the Sea," said the King. "We are happy to have a man from the country of Japan visit us."

The Princess of the Sea smiled

at Urashima. Urashima could not say a word. He could only look at the Princess, for he had never seen such a beautiful girl.

"You were kind to a turtle that was caught on your fish lines," said the Princess. "I was that turtle. I had changed myself into a turtle so that I could visit your country. You saved my life. And then I brought you down to the palace of the Sea so that you could meet my father."

The King of the Sea did everything he could to thank Urashima for saving his daughter's life.

Urashima was dressed in beautiful clothes. He was given jewels from the sea. He looked very handsome. Then there was feasting and dancing for many days.

Urashima and the Princess fell in love and were married. And the King of the Sea was very happy too.

Now there is no time in the magic that is under the sea. It is like one long summer day. The King of the Sea and the Princess never grow any older. Urashima enjoyed living in the palace of the Sea very much.

However, little by little Urashima began to think of his father and his mother. His father and his mother were getting old. Urashima had always been a good son and had looked after them. He wondered if they had enough fish to eat.

One day Urashima went to his beautiful wife and said,

"My dear wife, I must go back to my village. I must see if my father and my mother are well and happy."

"Will you come back to me?" asked the Princess.

"Oh, yes," said Urashima. "I love you better than anything in the world. I will come back to you as soon as I can."

Then the Princess gave Urashima a small box tied with a red silk string.

"When you look at this box, think of me," said the Princess. "But never, never open the box or you will never see me again."

"You have given me all the beautiful things that I have ever had in my life," said Urashima, as he took the box from the Princess.

"Remember to think of me when

you look at the box. But do not open the box," said the Princess.

"I will always think of you, my beautiful wife," said Urashima.

There were tears in the eyes of the Princess of the Sea. She did not want Urashima to go back to his country. But she knew that he would not be happy if he did not go back.

A giant turtle took Urashima back to his own country.

Urashima stood on the shore by his village. He waved goodbye to the giant turtle and thanked him for bringing him to his home.

Then Urashima looked around him. He saw the mountains behind the village. He saw the little river where he had kept his boat. But the village looked very strange.

The Return
of Urashima

Urashima returned to his village after living in the palace of the Sea King. He looked around, but everything looked strange.

Urashima walked through the streets of the village where he used to sell his fish. The houses looked different. The people looked different. Urashima had known every man, woman and child in the village when he left it. But now he saw no one that he knew. What had happened?

Urashima walked along the little river to the place where his father's house had stood. There was no house. But nearby was an old hut. In the door of the old hut stood an old, old woman.

"Old woman," said Urashima, "do you know where the Urashima family is living? They used to live in a house that stood by those trees on the bank of the river."

"I have never heard of the Urashima family," said the old woman. "And I am the only one who lives here on the bank of the river."

Urashima walked slowly back to the village. He could not understand what was the matter. He walked up and down the streets of the village, trying to find someone that he knew.

At last Urashima stopped an old, old man who was walking slowly along, holding on to a stick.

"Old man," asked Urashima, "can you tell me where the Urashima family is living?"

"Who are you?" asked the old man.

"I am Urashima Taro, and I have come to see my father and my mother."

The old man did not say a word for a long time.

"Have you never heard the story of Urashima Taro?" asked the old man. "My grandfather told me the story when I was a little boy. And his grandfather told him the story when he was a little boy. Urashima Taro went fishing one day and never returned to the village. His boat, with the fish lines still in it, came to the shore. But no one ever saw Urashima Taro again."

"His father and mother put a stone in the old graveyard just outside the village. And on the grave stone is written, 'Urashima Taro, drowned at sea.' His mother is buried on one side of the gravestone. And his father is buried on the other side of the gravestone."

"It is strange that a young man should ask me about Urashima Taro. He died more than two hundred years ago."

The old man stopped talking and walked slowly down the street. Urashima stood and watched him.

"There must be some magic that I do not understand," said Urashima to himself.

Then Urashima went out of the village to the old graveyard. He found his own gravestone. On it was written, "Urashima Taro, drowned at sea." And the gravestone was over two hundred years old.

"This cannot be true," said Urashima to himself. "I must find something that will help me to understand this matter."

Urashima walked down to the sea and sat on the sand. He looked over the beautiful sea. And then he thought of his wife.

"The Princess of the Sea will help me to understand what is the matter," he said to himself. He took from his pocket the little box that the Princess of the Sea had given to him.

"Perhaps my dear wife gave me this box so that I would understand," said Urashima to himself.

Then Urashima slowly took off the red silk string. He opened the box. Two jewels lay within the box. But before Urashima could touch the jewels, a white cloud came out of the box. It covered Urashima.

Urashima became old and old and old.

The people of the village found a very old man dead upon the sand by the sea.

The Goddess of Fuji

Mount Fuji is a very beautiful mountain. The people of Japan think that it is the most beautiful mountain in the world.

There are many stories about the goddess who lives on the top of Mount Fuji. And high up on the mountain there is a temple to this beautiful goddess.

Yosoji lived in a village at the foot of Mount Fuji. He loved the beautiful mountain with its snow top. The top of the mountain was as white as the camellias that grew in his mother's garden. And a white camellia is the whitest flower in the world.

One day Yosoji's mother became very sick. A great sickness had come to the village, and many people were sick. Yosoji was afraid that his mother was going to die.

Yosoji went to the magician and asked him for something to make his mother well. The magician said that he knew of no magic that would make his mother well again. But the magician said,

"Go up Mount Fuji. Go to the temple of the Goddess of Fuji and bring back the Water that Gives Life."

Now Yosoji had never climbed Mount Fuji before. Many older men in the village had tried to and some had even got to the top. But Yosoji knew that he must get the Water that Gives Life for his mother or she would die.

So Yosoji started to climb Mount Fuji. Up and up and up he climbed. He got so tired that he could hardly walk.

At last Yosoji got to a place where three paths met. He sat down to rest. And he prayed that he might take the right path and find for his mother the Water that Gives Life.

Suddenly a beautiful girl stood beside him. She was dressed all in white. She said, "Come with me."

Yosoji got up and followed the girl up the mountain. Soon they came to the temple. And by the temple was the stream of the Water that Gives Life.

"Yosoji, drink of the water," said the girl. "For you are near to death. Many older men have died before they have reached this stream."

Yosoji drank of the water. Then he felt much stronger, and he thanked the girl for coming to him and saving his life by showing him the way.

"Fill your gourd with the water," said the beautiful girl. "Take it to your mother. But in three days, come back. Your mother will need more of this water."

Yosoji filled his gourd with the water. He turned and carefully found his way back down the mountain. He got back to the village and he gave his mother a drink of the Water that Gives Life. And Yosoji gave some of the sick people in the village a drink of the water, too.

In three days, Yosoji started to climb Mount Fuji again. This time he carried a larger gourd, for there were many, many sick people in the village.

Yosoji came to the place where three paths met. The beautiful girl was waiting for him. She took him to the temple. And again Yosoji filled his gourd with the Water that Gives Life.

When Yosoji turned to thank the beautiful girl, she was gone. Then he started down the mountain again. He very carefully carried the gourd filled with the Water that Gives Life.

His mother and all the people of the village who drank of the water got well again.

The people thanked Yosoji. And they thanked the magician who sent Yosoji up Mount Fuji to find the Water that Gives Life.

But Yosoji knew in his heart that thanks should be given to the beautiful girl on Mount Fuji who had taken him to the temple. So Yosoji started to climb Mount Fuji again.

When Yosoji came to the place where three paths met, there was no one there to meet him. But this time he knew what path to take. And so he climbed on up to the temple.

Yosoji knelt beside the stream of the Water that Gives Life. He prayed that he might see the beautiful girl and thank her for making his mother well again.

When Yosoji looked up, there was a white cloud all around him. And floating in the white cloud, he could see the beautiful girl. In her hand she had a branch of white camellias.

The beautiful girl threw the branch of white camellias to

Yosoji. Then the white cloud
carried her to the top of Mount
Fuji, where the snow is as white
as the white camellias.

So Yosoji knew that the beautiful
girl who had helped him was the
Goddess of Fuji.

The Three Dwarf Trees

There was once a wise young man. He was a lord in Japan. He loved his people very much.

But the young lord heard that sometimes an officer of his court had not been kind to his people who were poor. This made the young lord very sad.

One day the young lord said to himself,

"I will put on the robes of a priest and go among the poor people. I will teach them to be good and kind to each other. And I will find out if the officers of my court are kind to them."

One night in the winter, the young lord, dressed as a priest, was walking toward a village. It began to snow, and the young lord became lost. At last he came to a poor man's hut. He knocked on the door of the hut.

The wife of the poor man opened the door of the hut. She saw a priest in his long robe standing in the snow.

"I have lost my way in the snow," said the priest, who was really the young lord. "Will you

please let me stay with you for
the night?"

"My husband is not at home,"
said the woman. "So I am sorry
that I cannot let you stay in our
hut tonight. But if you will go
down to that big tree, you will
find a road that leads to the
village."

The young lord went to the big
tree. There he met the husband
who was coming home from the
village.

"My good brother," said the
husband to the young lord, "Come
to my hut and stay tonight. The

snow is deep and it is a long way to the village."

So the young lord stayed that night with the poor man and his wife in their little hut.

The young lord ate supper with the man and his wife. There was little to eat, and he knew that the man and his wife must be poor indeed.

It was not very warm in the little hut. There was only one piece of wood burning on the fire. At last that one piece of wood was all burned up. And there was no more wood in the little hut.

The man went out into the garden, which was covered with snow. When he came back, he was carrying three pots. In the three pots were three dwarf trees.

Now in Japan a dwarf tree is worth a lot of money. The rich people like to have these dwarf trees in their houses. Sometimes a dwarf tree will be fifty years old, and it will be only about two feet tall.

The young lord knew that the poor man must at one time have been a rich man, or he would not have had three dwarf trees.

The man broke the dwarf trees into small pieces and put the pieces on the fire. Soon the little hut was warm again.

"My good brother must be warm when he stays the night with us," said the man, as he put the last piece of the dwarf trees on the fire.

The young lord talked with the man and his wife who lived in the poor little hut.

At last the poor man said,

"It is true that I am a samurai. I had much land and many fine houses."

Now a samurai is a nobleman in Japan. He serves his lord. And

when there is a war, he puts on
his armor and fights for his lord
and his country.

The young lord who was dressed
as a priest said,

"Why does a samurai and his
wife live in a poor little hut in
the country?"

"It is a sad story," said the
samurai. "Men from the North
with many servants came to my
house. They took my house and
lands. They turned my wife and
me out of our own house. I took
my armor and my horse. My wife
took three dwarf trees from our
beautiful garden. In the night we

went far away into the country where the men could not find us. We were afraid that they might kill us if they found us."

"Why do you not go to your lord and tell him your story. He would give your houses and your lands back to you. He would make those men go back to the North."

"The old lord has died," said the samurai. "And I am afraid that the young lord would not listen to the story of a poor countryman."

"I have heard that the young lord loves all of his people. I am

sure that he would help you," said
the young lord, who was dressed
as a priest.

"If the enemy comes to our
country, I will put on my armor
and go to the young lord," said
the samurai. "Then the young lord
will know that I am a samurai
and ready to fight for my country."

Then the wife spoke.

"Good brother, every night I
pray to the gods. I pray that some
day we will go back to our home."

"Some day the gods will answer
your prayer," said the young lord,
who was dressed as a priest.

The Young Lord

In the morning, the samurai opened the door of the little hut. Everything was covered with snow.

The wife cooked what little food she had for her husband and the young lord, who was dressed as a priest. And after breakfast, the young lord said,

"I must go now. I thank you for all your kindness. The gods will bring you many blessings."

"I will take you to the road that goes to the village," said the samurai.

So the young lord who was dressed as a priest went away.

The winter passed, and spring came. Springtime is the most beautiful time of the year in Japan. The cherry trees and the plum trees are covered with flowers.

But this springtime, an enemy came to Japan. The enemy was marching against the palace of the young lord.

The young lord sent messengers to all the samurai in his land.

"Put on your armor. Come to the palace at once and help drive the enemy from the country."

When the samurai who lived in the little hut in the country heard that an enemy was coming, he put on his armor. He said to his wife,

"I shall go to the palace of the lord. Then the lord will know that I am a samurai who will fight for his country."

The samurai got on his horse and rode to the palace. His horse looked very old. The samurai had no silk covers for his horse. His armor looked old.

When the samurai from the country rode up with the other samurai before the gates of the palace, he looked very, very shabby.

The gates of the palace opened and a messenger came through the gates. He came right up to the samurai from the country.

"Follow me," said the messenger.

The samurai from the country was much afraid. He was sure that the young lord would not let such a shabby samurai fight for his country.

But the samurai got off his horse and followed the messenger into the palace. The messenger took him to a large room where the young lord sat at a table.

The samurai bowed low to the floor. And when he looked up, he looked right into the face of the priest who had stayed all night in his poor hut in the wintertime.

The young lord spoke:

"You burned the most beautiful thing you had to keep me warm on a cold winter night. Do you remember?"

The samurai was so surprised that he could not say a word.

"When the enemy has been driven from our country," said the young lord, "you shall have your lands and your fine houses again. You are a good samurai."

How to Say Some Japanese Words

Words divided into syllables	How to say the syllables
Chu-go-ro	chŏŏ-gō-rō
Fu-ji	Fōō-jĭ
Hei-ta-ro	Hay-tah-rō
Hi-go	Hĭ-gō
Kyo-to	Kyō-tō
Mo-mo-ta-ro	Mō-mō-tah-rō
sam-u-rai	săm-ŏŏ-rī
U-ra-shi-ma	ŏŏ-rah-shĭ-mah
Yo-so-ji	Yō-sō-jĭ